THE MINDFUL MOTIVATIONAL JOURNEY

A DAILY DOSE OF POSITIVE THINKING

ANILKUMAR KOLAR RAMESH

Copyright © Anilkumar Kolar Ramesh
All Rights Reserved.

This book has been self-published with all reasonable efforts taken to make the material error-free by the author. No part of this book shall be used, reproduced in any manner whatsoever without written permission from the author, except in the case of brief quotations embodied in critical articles and reviews.

The Author of this book is solely responsible and liable for its content including but not limited to the views, representations, descriptions, statements, information, opinions and references ["Content"]. The Content of this book shall not constitute or be construed or deemed to reflect the opinion or expression of the Publisher or Editor. Neither the Publisher nor Editor endorse or approve the Content of this book or guarantee the reliability, accuracy or completeness of the Content published herein and do not make any representations or warranties of any kind, express or implied, including but not limited to the implied warranties of merchantability, fitness for a particular purpose. The Publisher and Editor shall not be liable whatsoever for any errors, omissions, whether such errors or omissions result from negligence, accident, or any other cause or claims for loss or damages of any kind, including without limitation, indirect or consequential loss or damage arising out of use, inability to use, or about the reliability, accuracy or sufficiency of the information contained in this book.

Made with ♥ on the Notion Press Platform
www.notionpress.com

To my dad, Mr. Ramesh K S, a retired teacher, and my mom, Ms. Radha J M, the pillars of my life: you are the reason for my existence in this world. Your unwavering love, support, and guidance have shaped me into the person I am today. This book is dedicated to you with heartfelt gratitude for your endless sacrifices and belief in my potential.

To my beautiful wife, Ms. Swathi P, my backbone and unwavering support: you have stood by my side through thick and thin, providing strength and encouragement when I needed it the most. Without you, it would not have been possible to write this book. Your love, understanding, and constant presence inspire me to reach new heights. This book is dedicated to you as a token of my love and appreciation.

I also want to express my deep appreciation to my paternal grandparents, Mr. Srinivasaiah R and Mrs. Lakshmamma R, and my maternal grandparents, Mr. Benghatta Munivenkatappa and Mrs. Lakshmamma R, for their blessings and wishes. Your love and support have been a source of strength.

To my loving family, who have been my constant source of love, support, and inspiration throughout this incredible journey: your unwavering belief in me and endless encouragement have fueled my passion for writing. This book is dedicated to each and every one of you as a heartfelt expression of gratitude for your presence in my life.

To my friends, thank you all for standing by me and being a source of laughter, joy, and encouragement. Your friendship has brought light and warmth into my life, and I am grateful for every shared moment and memory we have created.

To my mentors and teachers, thank you for guiding me, imparting your wisdom, and pushing me to reach for my full potential. Your guidance and expertise have been invaluable in shaping my writing and helping me grow as an author.

To the readers who embark on this literary journey, thank you for choosing to explore the pages of my book. I hope it brings you joy, inspiration, and moments of reflection. Your support and engagement mean the world to me, and I am humbled by the opportunity to share my words with you.

Finally, I dedicate this book to myself as a reminder of the strength, resilience, and determination that reside within me. May this dedication serve as a testament to the countless hours, the ups and downs, and the unwavering commitment I have poured into creating this book.

Contents

Contents

Preface

In the aftermath of the unprecedented pandemic that unfolded in 2020, our world was forever changed. Lives were lost, dreams were shattered, and uncertainty enveloped us all. Like countless others, I found myself caught in the storm, confronting the stark reality of a disrupted career and the weight of my shattered aspirations. Through the subsequent journey into darkness, I delved into the depths of despair and experienced the grip of depression.

Yet, within the chaos and desolation, a flicker of motivation ignited within me. It beckoned me to rise above, to defy the odds, and to embark on a transformative quest. Emerging from the abyss, I gained a newfound understanding—a realization that our world craves hope, inspiration, and unwavering motivation. It became evident that my own journey of self-discovery and resilience could serve as a guiding light for others.

This realization propelled me to pen the pages of "A Mindful Motivational Journey - A Daily Dose of Positive Thinking." In this book, I have gathered motivational thoughts and woven them together with stories—some derived from personal experience, and others crafted from imagination. It is a tale of triumph over adversity and the rekindling of dreams. Drawing upon my own battles with depression and the process of rebuilding my life, I offer practical strategies, profound reflections, and empowering affirmations to infuse your daily existence with positivity, mindfulness, and unwavering motivation.

Beyond the mere arrangement of words, this book embodies a testament to the extraordinary resilience of the human spirit. It implores you to embrace the profound power of positive thinking, to cultivate mindfulness in every facet of your life, and to reclaim agency over your own happiness and success. Within these pages, you will encounter a resounding reminder that no matter how far we may fall, we always possess the inner strength to rise again, fueled by an unwavering belief in our own potential.

My intention in crafting this book is to become your unwavering companion on this mindful motivational journey. I am here to walk alongside you, guiding you through the twists and turns of life, offering steadfast support, encouragement, and the tools necessary to rewrite the narratives that shape our existence. Together, let us transform each day into a tapestry woven with purpose, gratitude, and an unyielding commitment to personal growth.

Approach this book with an open mind, ready to embrace change, and allow its teachings to penetrate the depths of your heart, inspiring transformative actions and reshaping your perspective. May it serve as a constant reminder of your immense power to create a life brimming with joy, resilience, and unwavering positivity. As you embark on this journey through the pages of "A Mindful Motivational Journey - A Daily Dose of Positive Thinking," I extend my deepest gratitude for allowing me to be a part of your life's transformation. Together, let us rise above challenges, pursue our dreams with unwavering determination, and craft lives abundant with positivity and fulfillment.

With utmost sincerity and an unwavering belief in your potential.

Acknowledgements

Writing a book is a collaborative effort, and I am immensely grateful to all those who have contributed to the creation of "The Mindful Motivation Journey - A Daily Dose of Positive Thinking." Their support, guidance, and belief in this project have been instrumental in bringing it to fruition.

First and foremost, I would like to express my deepest appreciation to my family, which has been my constant source of love and encouragement. To my parents, Mr. Ramesh K S and Ms. Radha J M, thank you for instilling in me the values of perseverance and the pursuit of knowledge. Your unwavering support and belief in my abilities have been the driving force behind this book. To my beloved wife, Ms. Swathi P, thank you for standing by my side throughout this journey and for being my unwavering pillar of strength.

Last but not least, I would like to acknowledge the readers who have embraced "The Mindful Motivation Journey - A Daily Dose of Positive Thinking." Your support, engagement, and willingness to embark on this mindful journey have been the driving force behind my writing. It is your openness and curiosity that make this endeavor worthwhile.

To all those mentioned here and to those whose contributions may not be explicitly named but have been deeply felt, I extend my heartfelt gratitude. Your support, whether big or small, has made this book possible. I am honored and humbled to have you in my life.

CHAPTER ONE

DAY 1

"UNTIL YOU CROSS THE BRIDGE OF INSECURITIES, YOU CAN'T BEGIN TO EXPLORE POSSIBILITIES."

The bridge of insecurities stands between us and our potential. Crossing it is the first step to unlocking possibilities. Confronting doubts and fears opens the door to growth, learning, and new experiences. Embracing vulnerability is key to discovering uncharted territories within ourselves and realizing the vast potential that lies beyond our comfort zones.

In the tranquil village of Ramavaram, there lived a girl named Suma, whose heart yearned for the vastness beyond the boundaries of her close-knit community. However, her aspirations were overshadowed by formidable obstacles—her own overwhelming fears.

Every day, Suma found herself drawn to the sturdy bridge that connected her village to the unknown. It beckoned with the promise of extraordinary adventures, yet her deep-seated anxieties held her back, like invisible chains.

One radiant morning, a surge of determination coursed through Suma. With trembling legs and a heart drumming with anticipation, she stepped onto the bridge. The old structure swayed and creaked beneath her, intensifying her fears. Yet, she pressed on, fixing her gaze on the unseen horizons.

As Suma traversed the bridge, her fears began to dissipate. What was once a source of terror transformed into a symbol of her newfound courage. Upon reaching the other side, she was met with a world that surpassed her wildest dreams—a world bursting with opportunities she had never fathomed within the confines of her village.

Suma's journey became a profound metaphor for life. It illustrated that to truly experience the richness life had to offer, one had to confront internal fears and cross metaphorical bridges. Empowered by her newfound courage, Suma felt ready to embrace not only the external world but also the uncharted territories of her own doubts and insecurities.

Her story resonated deeply within the village, becoming a source of inspiration. It taught the villagers that confronting fears was the key to unlocking boundless possibilities. Suma, once bound by the limitations of her own apprehensions, had become a living testament to the transformative power of courage. Her journey echoed the universal truth that beyond every bridge of fear lies a realm of untapped potential waiting to be explored.

CHAPTER TWO

DAY 2

"THE MOST DETERMINATIVE AND MOTIVATING SENTENCE WHICH SHOULD ALWAYS BE FOLLOWED IN LIFE. The RACE IS NOT OVER BECAUSE I HAVEN'T WON YET."

This motivational sentence encapsulates the essence of perseverance. It echoes the idea that life is an ongoing journey, and challenges are opportunities for growth. By acknowledging that the race isn't over until victory, it encourages a resilient mindset, continuous effort, and the unwavering belief that every setback is a step towards ultimate success.

In the serene outskirts of a small town, there resided Raju, a dedicated runner. His story unfolded with a setback, an early stumble in the race of life. Yet, at each finish line, a profound mantra echoed within him: "The race is not over because I haven't won yet."

Life dealt Raju losses, but this mantra became his beacon. A pivotal moment approached – a major race. Just as victory seemed near, a searing pain shot through Raju's legs. Doubt crept in, threatening to overshadow his spirit. However, the persistent echo of his mantra surged louder.

Summoning a reservoir of determination, Raju pressed on. The finish line was crossed, not as the first but as someone triumphant. The crowd erupted in cheers, acknowledging the spirit that transcended mere competition. In that moment, Raju grasped a profound truth – the true race wasn't against others; it was an internal journey of self-discovery and growth.

This mantra, etched in his heart, had been his steadfast companion, propelling him through life's challenges. It taught him that victory isn't confined to reaching a finish line; it's about embracing the perpetual race of becoming the best version of oneself.

CHAPTER THREE

DAY 3

"TALENTS WILL TAKE US TO HIGH POSITION IN OUR CAREER. BUT BEHAVIOUR WILL HELP US TO MAINTAIN THE HIGH POSITION IN HEARTS OF OTHERS."

While talents propel us to success, it's our behavior that sustains it. Achieving a high position in our career requires skills, but maintaining that position in others' hearts demands positive conduct. How we treat others, communicate, and collaborate shapes enduring impressions, fostering meaningful relationships that extend beyond professional achievements.

In the dynamic realm of technology, Sahana emerged as a luminary. Her coding prowess and innovative thinking swiftly elevated her to a coveted position within the buzzing confines of her workplace. However, it wasn't merely Sahana's technical brilliance that set her apart; it was the whispering tales of her genuine success spun by her behavior.

Sahana's reputation extended beyond lines of code; she was equally renowned for her humility and empathy. In the collaborative arena of her workplace, she was not just a technical expert but a beacon of warmth and encouragement. Sahana generously shared her knowledge, mentored her colleagues, and reveled in collective achievements, creating a vibrant atmosphere that transcended the usual confines of a tech-centric environment.

Then came a critical project, laden with unexpected challenges. It was in these testing times that Sahana's true character illuminated the office. Instead of resorting to blame or pointing fingers, she rallied her team, fostering unity and inspiring them to surmount obstacles together. In the face of adversity, her behavior resonated louder than any meticulously crafted code.

While Sahana's exceptional talents had catapulted her to the zenith of her career, it was her behavior, marked by an authentic concern for her team, that etched her indelibly into the hearts of others. Her success story, therefore, wasn't confined to the summits of professional achievement but extended into the valleys of compassion, making Sahana's narrative truly unforgettable.

DAY 4

"IF WE REALIZE OUR QUALITIES, WE BECOME SMART. IF WE KNOW OUR WEAKNESSES, WE BECOME INTELLIGENT. AND IF WE ARE AWARE OF OUR QUALITIES AS WELL AS OUR WEAKNESSES, WE BECOME SUCCESSFUL."

Understanding oneself is a profound journey. Recognition of our strengths leads to wisdom, shaping us into smart individuals. Acknowledging our weaknesses signifies intelligence, fostering growth and resilience. Yet, true success unfolds when we navigate both, harnessing strengths and addressing weaknesses, creating a holistic self-awareness that becomes the cornerstone of genuine success.

In the serene town of Reflection, Maya embarked on a profound journey of self-discovery. Unveiling her strengths, a newfound confidence molded her into a discerning and capable individual. However, Maya did not refrain from delving into her vulnerabilities. With each challenge, she demonstrated remarkable intelligence, turning setbacks into opportunities for growth.

Maya's narrative truly blossomed as she embraced both her strengths and weaknesses. Armed with self-awareness, she embarked on a venture, navigating the intricacies of success. Reflection, symbolizing her personal evolution, bore witness to Maya's triumphs and falls, each contributing to her unique symphony of success.

Her story resonated beyond the town, becoming an inspiration for others. Maya's harmonious blend of qualities and vulnerabilities illustrated that genuine success arises not just from strengths but from a profound understanding of one's entire self. In the town of Reflection, Maya's tale became a guiding light, encouraging others on their own odyssey of self-discovery and triumph.a

CHAPTER FIVE

DAY 5

"LIFE IS VERY SIMILAR TO A BOXING RING. DEFEAT IS NOT DECLARED WHEN YOU FALL DOWN. IT'S DECLARED WHEN YOU REFUSE TO RISE UP..!!"

Life mirrors a boxing ring; the match isn't lost when you hit the canvas; it's conceded when the will to stand eludes you. In the face of setbacks, it's not the stumble that defines, but the resilience to rise that marks the true triumph. Life's essence lies in the relentless pursuit despite the knocks, where victory is scripted not by avoiding falls but by the courage to stand tall again.

In the bustling city of Metropolis, Ram Raj, an aspiring boxer, entered the ring of life with dreams and determination. One day, an unexpected defeat left him sprawled on the canvas. The arena fell silent, but the bell, rather than signaling surrender, echoed with the promise of a second chance.

Bruised and humbled, Ram Raj refused to be broken. Each fall became a stepping stone, a lesson etched into the fabric of his resilience. Life's challenges intensified when a formidable opponent, named Adversity, emerged.

Struggling against the relentless blows, Ram Raj found himself on the canvas once more.

In that critical moment, the referee's count mirrored Ram Raj's indomitable resolve. With a surge of determination, he rose, transforming defeat's whispers into a roar of courage. The match continued, but Ram Raj's refusal to stay down shifted the narrative. The final bell rang, not marking a flawless victory, but a triumph over adversity.

The crowd erupted in applause, recognizing that in life's unrelenting ring, defeat isn't measured by the fall; it's a conscious choice to remain down. Ram Raj, with unwavering courage, chose to rise again, scripting a story that echoed far beyond the confines of the boxing arena.

CHAPTER SIX

DAY 6

"JOURNEY OF LIFE IS EXCITING WHEN YOU CHALLENGE YOUR OWN WEAKNESSESS. SOMETIMES, YOUR ENEMY TEACHES YOU. BETTER THAN YOUR FRIEND. ACEPT EVERY CHALLENGE POSITIVELY."

Life's journey becomes thrilling when you confront your own weaknesses. In the face of challenges, adversaries can become unexpected teachers, offering lessons that friends might not provide. Embrace each challenge with a positive outlook, viewing them as opportunities for growth and self-discovery. It's in these moments of adversity that your true strengths emerge, shaping a resilient and enlightened version of yourself. Every challenge, every encounter, becomes a stepping stone on the exciting path of self-improvement and personal evolution.

In the picturesque town of Kolar, where the whispers of nature intertwined with the aspirations of its residents, Sonika, a budding artist, embarked on the canvas of life with dreams as vivid as her palette. Her journey, akin to an artwork in progress, unfolded with both vibrant hues and subtle shadows.

Sonika faced an unexpected challenge in the form of a professional rival, Serena. Initially perceived as an adversary, Serena's critiques became a surprising source of enlightenment. Instead of letting competition breed animosity, Sonika chose to extract valuable lessons from her supposed enemy.

Sonika's studio became a haven of transformation. Each brushstroke carried the weight of self-discovery as she navigated not only the strokes of success but also the intricate details of her own insecurities. Embracing challenges with a positive spirit, Sonika turned each obstacle into an opportunity to refine her technique.

As her canvas filled with the dynamic interplay of colors, friendships, and rivalries, Sonika's art mirrored the beauty of resilience. In the end, the enemy's teachings, initially unexpected but profound, guided her toward mastery. Kolar witnessed not just the evolution of an artist but the creation of a masterpiece, proving that challenges, when accepted with positivity, can transform weaknesses into strokes of brilliance on the canvas of life.

DAY 7

"ALMOST EVERYTHING CAN BE PURCHASED AT A REDUCED PRICE, EXPECT OUR SATISFACTION. THAT'S LIFE."

Life, in its intricate marketplace, offers discounts on almost everything, but satisfaction remains priceless. Amidst the bargains and sales, the currency of contentment doesn't diminish. It's a commodity beyond the reach of mere transactions, a treasure uniquely crafted in the moments of genuine joy, accomplishment, and connection. No clearance tag adorns the aisle of fulfillment; it's woven into the fabric of experiences and the tapestry of relationships. In this grand emporium of existence, where the cost of material possessions fluctuates, the value of true satisfaction remains constant. It's a poignant reminder that the richness of life isn't measured by what we acquire at a discount but by the depth of joy and contentment that money can't buy.

In the bustling city of Mumbai, where the rhythm of life resonates through crowded streets and towering skyscrapers, lived Kumar, a diligent young man with dreams as vast as the Arabian Sea that embraced the city.

His days were woven with the tapestry of ambition, as he navigated through the labyrinth of opportunities that Mumbai offered.

Kumar, however, understood that in the cacophony of ambition, the symphony of satisfaction often played a muted tune. Mumbai, with its glittering skyline, whispered tales of success, but Kumar yearned for a currency more profound than wealth—a currency that could not be bargained for in the city's bustling markets.

As Kumar traversed the varied landscapes of Mumbai, from the vibrant markets of Colaba to the quietude of Marine Drive, he encountered a multitude of characters, each with their own pursuits. Yet, amid the hustle, he discovered that the price of genuine satisfaction was not listed on any stock exchange.

In the city's renowned Dabbawala system, where efficiency was a celebrated art, Kumar found a subtle metaphor for life. The famed Dabbawalas, despite carrying tiffin boxes filled with the flavors of Mumbai, understood that the true essence of their work was not merely delivering lunches. It was about nourishing connections, about adding a dash of care to the daily grind of the city.

Inspired, Kumar began to redefine success in the context of his own life. While the city clamored for material achievements, Kumar sought a different kind of wealth—the wealth of meaningful relationships, the richness of experiences that transcended the confines of a balance sheet.

In the narrow alleys of Dharavi, Mumbai's largest slum, Kumar encountered individuals who, with meager resources, crafted dreams larger than life. Their resilience spoke volumes—their satisfaction not derived from material abundance but from a profound appreciation for the simple joys that life offered.

Kumar's journey through Mumbai became a pilgrimage of self-discovery. He realized that almost everything in the city could be purchased at a reduced price, but genuine satisfaction was not a commodity found in the markets; it was a jewel discovered in the depth of human connections, in the simplicity of shared moments, and in the pursuit of a purpose that extended beyond the glittering skyline.

As Kumar stood by the shores of Marine Drive, gazing at the city's skyline glittering against the canvas of a setting sun, he understood that life's true bargains were hidden in the everyday interactions, in the laughter shared with friends, and in the moments of quiet reflection amidst the chaos.

Mumbai, with all its grandeur, had become Kumar's teacher. It taught him that satisfaction, unlike the tangible possessions in the city's markets, couldn't be bought or sold. It had to be earned through the investments of kindness, the dividends of meaningful relationships, and the capital of a purposeful existence.

In the end, as Kumar continued his journey through the vibrant tapestry of Mumbai, he carried with him not just the dreams of success but the invaluable currency of genuine satisfaction—a treasure that no price tag could define, and no discount could diminish. In the city that never sleeps, Kumar had found the elusive jewel that made every step of his journey worthwhile—the priceless satisfaction that breathed life into his ambitions and illuminated the bustling city with a glow that transcended the glittering lights of its skyline.

CHAPTER EIGHT

DAY 8

"FIND THAT PERSON WHO WILL PICK UP EVERY PIECE OF YOUR SHATTERED HEART & PUT IT BACK TOGETHER; REPLACING IT WITH A PIECE OF HIS/HER."

Discover that person who becomes the gentle healer of your fractured heart, picking up every shattered piece with care and devotion. In the delicate act of reconstruction, they don't just mend; they replace the broken fragments with pieces of their own. This profound connection is a symbiotic exchange, where love becomes the mender, and hearts intertwine in a shared tapestry of healing. It's in this reciprocity that the true magic of profound connections unfolds, creating a bond that goes beyond repairing what's broken, leaving both hearts forever changed by the exchange.

In the vibrant town of Suryapura, where the air was perpetually kissed by the fragrance of blossoms, Bajarang, a humble florist, cultivated more than just flowers. His small shop, adorned with vivid petals, became a haven for the townsfolk seeking solace and respite from the bustling world outside. Bajarang, with hands seasoned by the earth, not only arranged flowers but also wove tales of hope within the delicate petals.

As the seasons changed, so did the stories whispered within the blossoms. Bajarang's generosity extended beyond mere blooms; he offered an attentive ear to sorrows and a soothing balm for troubled hearts. Amidst the fragrant symphony of roses and lilies, friendships blossomed like buds unfurling in the warmth of shared moments.

One day, a weary traveler, burdened with the weight of untold stories, entered the welcoming enclave of Suryapura. Bajarang, with an uncanny ability to sense tales etched in the lines of the stranger's face, presented a vibrant bouquet. The traveler's eyes lit up with a spark of gratitude, and in that simple exchange, Bajarang discovered the magic of sharing not just flowers but the transformative power of empathy.

In the heart of Suryapura, Bajarang's name echoed not just as a florist but as a cultivator of compassion. His small shop became a sanctuary where the language of flowers spoke of more than just beauty—it spoke of shared joys, sorrows, and the universal human experience. Bajarang, the humble cultivator of both blooms and kindness, enriched the vibrant town with the enduring fragrance of empathy, turning Suryapura into a haven where every petal whispered tales of compassion and every bouquet held the magic of shared humanity.

CHAPTER NINE

DAY 9

"BEST PART OF OUR LIFE IS WHEN OUR FAMILY UNDERSTANDS US AS A FRIEND AND OUR FRIEND SUPPORTS US AS FAMILY."

The sweetest chapter of our existence unfolds when our family evolves into understanding friends, and our friends transform into steadfast family. In this beautiful synchronicity, kinship transcends traditional bounds, and friendships deepen into bonds as unyielding as blood ties. The magic lies in the mutual understanding between family members, where conversations flow seamlessly, and support becomes an unspoken promise. Simultaneously, our chosen friends stand as pillars, offering the unwavering support and unconditional love typically associated with family. This harmonious dance between familial understanding and friendly solidarity creates a tapestry of connection, wherein the distinctions between family and friends blur, leaving us surrounded by a network of cherished souls who comprehend us as both kin and kindred spirits.

In the serene village of Ramavaram, where the air carried the fragrance of earth and the days unfolded at a pace dictated by the sun, lived Naziya. Her life was a canvas painted with the simplicity and warmth that only a close-knit village community could offer.

Naziya's family, a tapestry of connections, were not just relatives; they were companions in the intricate journey of life. In the heart of Ramavaram, their days were woven with shared laughter around the dinner table, and their nights found solace in the comfort of each other's presence.

However, among the threads of familial bonds, Naziya's closest confidante wasn't a family member but her childhood friend, Aryan. Their friendship, nurtured in the golden afternoons of Ramavaram, stood as a testament to the enduring nature of connections made in the simplicity of village life. Aryan, though not bound by blood, was embraced by Naziya's family as if he had always been one of their own.

As the sun dipped below the horizon, painting vibrant hues over Ramavaram's fields, Naziya's life unfolded like a beautifully written story of unity. In this village tapestry, where every villager was a thread, familial bonds stretched beyond the confines of blood ties, and friendships blossomed into relationships as resilient as family.

Ramavaram, in all its simplicity, held the profound truth that family isn't merely about shared DNA; it's about the hearts we choose to include in our stories. It's about the threads of love, understanding, and shared experiences that bind us all together, turning the village into a sanctuary of belonging where every villager was a cherished part of the tale of Ramavaram.

CHAPTER TEN

DAY 10

"GREAT ATTITUDE FOR LIFE - "IT'S TRUE THAT I AM NOT PERFECT IN MANY THINGS. BUT EVEN THIS IS TRUE THAT MANY THINGS ARE NOT PERFECT WITHOUT ME." BELIEVE IN YOURSELF."

This attitude champions self-belief by affirming imperfection while highlighting the indispensable role each person plays. It's a declaration that, despite personal flaws, one contributes uniquely to the world. This belief nurtures resilience, fostering a positive mindset that recognizes individual worth. It's an acknowledgment that the intricacies of life are incomplete without the distinct imprint of each person. This mantra encourages confidence, urging individuals to navigate challenges with the understanding that their presence is not just valuable but, in fact, essential to the imperfect yet harmonious symphony of existence.

In the tranquil embrace of Godavari, a town where time seemed to dance at a leisurely pace, lived Ravulamma, a beacon of spirited resilience. Her infectious smile, undeterred by a rare condition, painted the town with the hues of her indomitable spirit. One fateful day, Ravulamma stumbled upon an abandoned garden, a forgotten canvas yearning for life.

With a heart fueled by unwavering determination, Ravulamma rallied the villagers to join her quest. Together, they embarked on a transformative journey, their hands tilling the soil, breathing life into the forgotten earth. The metamorphosis was nothing short of magical. The once-neglected garden burst forth, a riot of colors as if nature itself rejoiced in the revival.

Godavari, through this kaleidoscopic transformation, became a living testament to Ravulamma's profound belief — imperfections are the seeds of unique beauty. The garden, much like its guardian, stood as a living metaphor, radiating vibrancy and proving that many things in this tranquil town were not perfect without Ravulamma's touch.

In the gentle embrace of Godavari, Ravulamma's story unfolded as more than just the rejuvenation of a garden; it became a symbol of unity, resilience, and the extraordinary beauty that blossoms when imperfections are embraced. The once-forgotten garden turned into a haven where the community found solace, a place where the tapestry of flaws and vibrant colors harmonized into a mosaic of collective strength and shared beauty. And in this symphony of transformation, Ravulamma's indomitable spirit echoed, reminding everyone that true beauty lies not in perfection but in the celebration of life's imperfections.

CHAPTER ELEVEN

DAY 11

"NEVER STOP DOING OUR BEST JUST BECAUSE SOMEONE DOESN'T UNDERSTAND IT. WE NEED TO DO OUR BEST FOR OUR SATISFACTION, NOT FOR OTHERS' APPROVAL."

Persist in giving your best, even if others fail to comprehend your efforts. The driving force should be personal satisfaction, not external validation. In a world where understanding varies, commitment to excellence becomes an intrinsic journey. By doing our best for personal fulfillment, the emphasis shifts from seeking approval to cultivating a sense of accomplishment. This mantra empowers self-driven perseverance, fostering resilience against external judgments. Ultimately, the intrinsic reward of personal satisfaction becomes the compass guiding endeavors, reminding us that the true measure of success lies in our commitment to excellence, irrespective of external perceptions.

In the cultural heart of Mysore, Sarvesh, a soul adorned with artistic fervor, painted his world with hues that transcended convention. His creations, though perplexing to the locals, echoed the heartbeat of his passion. Unyielding to the puzzled glances, Sarvesh continued to wield his brush with an unwavering spirit.

One fateful day, a wandering art critic descended upon Mysore, dismissing Sarvesh's work as beyond comprehension. Unfazed, Sarvesh sought refuge in his creative sanctum, a space where the strokes of his imagination danced freely. Little did he know, the enchantment of his dedication stirred the souls of the locals, awakening an appreciation for the distinct beauty embedded in his art.

Mysore, once a tapestry of traditional tastes, transformed into an art-loving haven where Sarvesh's canvases sparked a revolution of expression. The city's narrow alleys and grand boulevards echoed with the symphony of diverse artistic voices. Sarvesh's narrative emerged as a testament to the resounding mantra: "Never stop doing our best just because someone doesn't understand it."

The pages of Mysore's artistic story turned, revealing that what was initially misunderstood became the hallmark of individuality. Sarvesh's art, once shrouded in perplexity, unfurled as a symbol of authenticity. The city learned that true satisfaction lay not in conforming to external expectations but in the unbridled expression of one's unique vision.

As Mysore embraced the kaleidoscope of artistic diversity, Sarvesh stood as a living testament, reminding all that genuine fulfillment is found in the unwavering pursuit of one's creative truth, irrespective of the symphony of external opinions. The once-misunderstood artist became the maestro, orchestrating a transformative melody that resonated through the cultural corridors of Mysore, immortalizing the mantra that had guided his journey.

CHAPTER TWELVE

DAY 12

"IT'S NOT VERY HARD TO SACRIFICE EVERYTHING FOR SOMEONE. BUT IT'S HARD TO FIND SOMEONE WHO RESPECTS YOUR SACRIFICE..!!"

Sacrificing for someone comes naturally, but finding someone who genuinely respects and acknowledges those sacrifices is a rarity. The quote underscores the emotional depth of selfless giving and the importance of reciprocity in relationships. It implies that the true challenge lies not in the act of sacrificing itself but in discovering a person who values and respects the sacrifices made on their behalf. It serves as a poignant reminder that mutual respect in the face of sacrifice forms the foundation of meaningful connections, emphasizing the significance of a two-way understanding and gratitude in the dynamics of genuine relationships.

In the serene town of Tumkur, where time moved at its own unhurried pace, lived a man named Harishchandra. His days were woven with threads of simple joys and acts of kindness that became the heartbeat of the community.

Harishchandra, despite facing his share of life's storms, was a beacon of compassion. His deeds, like ripples in a pond, touched every corner of Tumkur. One fine day, a stranger named Arjun arrived, seeking refuge in the town's warmth. Harishchandra, without a second thought, extended his hand in friendship, leaving an indelible mark on Arjun's heart.

Deeply moved by Harishchandra's selflessness, Arjun felt the urge to express his gratitude. With the cooperation of the townsfolk, he planned a surprise celebration in Harishchandra's honor. As the sun dipped below the hills, the quiet town of Tumkur came alive with laughter, music, and the warm glow of shared appreciation.

Harishchandra, a humble soul, was oblivious to the gathering. When he stepped into the adorned square, he found himself enveloped in the warmth of a community united by gratitude. Tears welled in his eyes as he realized that, indeed, it's not very hard to sacrifice everything for someone, but it's hard to find someone who respects your sacrifice.

Tumkur, on that memorable day, transformed into a canvas painted with the hues of selflessness and appreciation. The townsfolk, inspired by Harishchandra's unwavering kindness, embraced the philosophy that genuine acknowledgment can transform simple acts of sacrifice into a symphony of shared gratitude. As the stars adorned the night sky, Tumkur stood not just as a town but as a testament to the enduring power of kindness and the beauty of recognizing and respecting each other's sacrifices.

CHAPTER THIRTEEN

DAY 13

"IT'S OKAY TO CARE ABOUT WHAT PEOPLE THINK. BUT THERE'S A DIFFERENCE BETWEEN VALUING SOMEONE'S OPINION AND NEEDING THEIR APPROVAL."

Caring about others' opinions is natural, but it's crucial to distinguish between valuing their input and seeking approval. While valuing opinions can offer diverse perspectives and insights, the need for constant approval may lead to a compromised sense of self. It's important to strike a balance, acknowledging external viewpoints without allowing them to dictate one's identity. True confidence stems from self-acceptance and understanding, allowing room for growth while maintaining authenticity. Embracing the difference between caring for opinions and needing approval fosters a healthy sense of self-worth and autonomy in navigating life's complexities.

In the historic city of Bijapura, Suchitra, an ardent historian, delved into the ancient tales etched in its monuments. As she navigated through the ruins, a mysterious artifact caught her eye. Enthralled, Suchitra embarked on an archaeological journey, uncovering forgotten stories.

Her discoveries sparked the interest of the academic community, attracting both admiration and skepticism. Amidst the scholarly debates, Suchitra's passion and dedication shone. She transformed Bijapura into a living testament of her love for history.

However, challenges loomed when a rival scholar contested her findings. Undeterred, Suchitra meticulously defended her research. The academic clash echoed through Bijapura, but Suchitra's commitment resonated louder.

As the dust settled, Suchitra emerged victorious. Her perseverance not only enriched Bijapura's historical narrative but also exemplified that in the pursuit of knowledge, resilience is the key to unlocking the hidden treasures of the past. Suchitra's name echoed through the ancient stones, forever intertwining her legacy with the soul of Bijapura.

CHAPTER FOURTEEN

DAY 14

"IF YOU WANT TO KNOW SOMEONE'S MIND, LISTEN TO THEIR WORDS. IF YOU WANT TO KNOW THEIR HEART, WATCH THEIR ACTIONS."

Understanding a person requires more than just hearing their words. Words can be a facade, while actions unveil the true intentions and emotions. Someone's genuine self is reflected not in what they say but in how they act. Observing actions provides insights into the sincerity, values, and emotions that lie within. Actions are the unfiltered expression of one's character, revealing the authentic essence that words may conceal. In relationships and interactions, paying attention to actions allows a deeper comprehension of individuals beyond the surface, fostering genuine connections built on understanding and authenticity.

In the vibrant state of Tamil Nadu, within the culturally rich tapestry of history, lived Selvaraj, a storyteller whose tales resonated through the ancient temples and bustling cities. His narratives weren't just stories; they were windows into the soul of Tamil Nadu.

Selvaraj, with his animated expressions and vivid words, transported listeners across time. His stories embraced the state's iconic landmarks, like the Meenakshi Amman Temple and the rock-cut temples of Mahabalipuram, weaving them into sagas of love, valor, and architectural marvels. Locals gathered in the evening, captivated by his ability to breathe life into the stones that stood as silent witnesses to centuries.

One fateful day, an outsider named Arjun visited Tamil Nadu. Intrigued by Selvaraj's tales, he joined the enthralled audience. As the sun dipped below the horizon, Selvaraj narrated a story that transcended time, bridging the gap between the ancient and the contemporary.

His words resonated with Arjun, sparking a connection between past and present. Inspired, Arjun proposed a collaborative project to document Tamil Nadu's stories. Selvaraj, recognizing the opportunity to preserve his beloved state's legacy, enthusiastically agreed.

Together, they embarked on a journey to immortalize Tamil Nadu's tales. Through meticulous research, vibrant storytelling, and Arjun's artistic touch, they created an anthology that breathed life into the state's history.

Tamil Nadu, through the collaborative efforts of Selvaraj and Arjun, became not just a region on the map but a living narrative, where the past intertwined seamlessly with the present. The tapestry of Tamil Nadu's stories, once whispered through the ages, now echoed loudly, resonating in the hearts of those who called it home and those who had just discovered its enchanting tales.

In the heart of Tamil Nadu, the ancient temples whispered their gratitude to Selvaraj, the storyteller who, with Arjun's help, had given them a voice that would endure for generations.

DAY 15

"RELATIONS ARE SIMILAR TO A DICTIONARY, IT PROVIDES MEANING & EXPLANATIONS ONLY TO THOSE WHO REFER IT PROPERLY."

Relationships, much like a dictionary, unfold their depth when approached with sincere understanding. They offer profound meanings and explanations to those who navigate them with care and attention. Just as one delves into a dictionary to comprehend the nuances of words, delving into relationships with empathy and patience unveils the layers of emotions and connections. The true essence of any relationship is revealed not through superficial glances but through a sincere exploration, much like a reader seeking comprehension in the pages of a well-used dictionary.

In the vibrant city of Madras, Namitha, a seasoned storyteller, embarked on an enchanting narrative of human connections. Her tales, woven with the rich tapestry of Tamil Nadu, reflected the diverse hues of relationships.

Namitha's stories transcended the ordinary, exploring the intricacies of human bonds. One narrative revolved around Suchitra, a spirited young woman navigating the bustling streets of Bijapur. As Namitha unfolded her journey, the audience found themselves immersed in the tapestry of her relationships — familial warmth, friendships blossoming like the fragrant jasmine in the temples, and the subtle dance of love in the midst of bustling markets.

Through Namitha's narratives, the audience discovered that, much like a well-compiled dictionary, relationships offered meaning and explanations to those who approached them with respect and understanding. The depth and beauty of human connections unfolded, painting the canvas of life with the myriad emotions and experiences that make each relationship unique.

In this cultural symphony, the city of Madras echoed with the resonance of Namitha's stories, each chapter revealing that the true essence of relationships lies in the heartfelt exploration of their meanings and the connections they bring to our lives.

CHAPTER SIXTEEN

DAY 16

"A SEED GROWS WITH NO SOUND, BUT A TREE FALLS WITH HUGE NOISE. DESTRUCTION HAS NOISE, BUT CREATION IS QUIET. THIS IS THE POWER OF SILENCE. "GROW SILENTLY..!!"

In the profound simplicity of silence lies the essence of creation. The quiet growth of a seed into a towering tree symbolizes the potency of silent progress. While destruction makes noise, creation, in its transformative journey, thrives in silence. It's a reminder that real growth doesn't always announce itself but unfolds quietly. Embracing the power of silence allows one to nurture inner strength, resilience, and the ability to weather storms without unnecessary noise. The wisdom lies in growing silently, steadily, and authentically, a testament to the impactful force concealed within the stillness of progress.

n the serene village of Sompura, where time seemed to flow at a gentler pace, there lived Namitha. She was known for her quiet strength, much like the village itself, where whispers of the wind and rustling leaves were the only sounds that broke the tranquility.

Namitha, a teacher in the village school, had a unique way of connecting with her students. Instead of loud commands, she used the power of silence to capture their attention. She believed that, like the gentle growth of the crops in Sompura's fields, knowledge too could flourish in a quiet, nurturing environment.

One day, a group of urban educators visited Sompura. Expecting a bustling classroom, they were surprised to find Namitha's students engrossed in their studies with serene concentration. The power of Namitha's teaching wasn't in loud instructions but in the quiet understanding she cultivated.

As the visitors witnessed the harmonious relationship between the teacher, students, and the peaceful village surroundings, they left with a newfound appreciation for the strength that lies in silence. Sompura became a symbol of the profound impact that can be achieved through quiet growth and thoughtful nurturing, both in education and life.

CHAPTER SEVENTEEN

DAY 17

"SUCCESS FOCUSES ON THE SIX D'S: DESIRE, DETERMINATION, DISCIPLINE, DEVOTION, DEDICATION & DESTINY."

Success is a culmination of six essential elements encapsulated in the six D's. First, Desire fuels the journey, acting as the driving force. Determination ensures resilience, overcoming obstacles with unwavering commitment. Discipline instills the necessary habits and structure for progress. Devotion signifies wholehearted dedication to the chosen path. Dedication amplifies the efforts, translating aspirations into consistent action. Lastly, Destiny represents the culmination of these factors, the ultimate realization of one's goals. Together, these six D's form a holistic framework, guiding individuals through the intricate journey of achieving success, underscoring the significance of passion, persistence, structure, commitment, and the belief in a destined outcome.

Once upon a time in the serene village of Kanchana Ganga, there lived a curious young girl named Usha. She harbored an insatiable desire for exploration and knowledge. One day, while wandering through the ancient forest bordering Kanchana Ganga, Usha stumbled upon a hidden cave entrance. Undeterred by the ominous darkness within, she entered.

Inside, she discovered an enchanted book that shimmered with ethereal light. The book revealed the secrets of the "Grove Guardians," mythical creatures tasked with protecting the balance of nature. Usha felt an inexplicable connection to these guardians and pledged to help them when an ominous shadow threatened Kanchana Ganga.

As the days passed, Usha honed her skills, embracing determination and discipline. She showed devotion to the guardians and dedicated herself to understanding the ancient wisdom within the book. The villagers, skeptical at first, witnessed Usha's transformation and rallied behind her.

When the shadow finally emerged, a menacing force threatening Kanchana Ganga, Usha confronted it with unwavering courage. The Grove Guardians, sensing her commitment, joined forces. Through a harmonious blend of Usha's newfound abilities and the guardians' ancient magic, they vanquished the shadow, restoring peace to Kanchana Ganga.

Usha's journey, guided by destiny, not only saved her village but also illuminated the interconnectedness of desire, determination, discipline, devotion, dedication, and destiny. The enchanted book closed, its pages filled with the tale of a young girl named Usha who, against all odds, became the bridge between two worlds, proving that within the heart of a dreamer lies the power to shape destiny. And so, in the serene village of Kanchana Ganga, a new chapter began, echoing the triumph of one girl's extraordinary journey.

CHAPTER EIGHTEEN

DAY 18

"WELL-WISHER IS NOT A WORD. NOT MERELY A RELATIONSHIP. IT IS A SILENT PROMISE WHICH SAYS, I WAS, I AM, & I WILL BE WITH YOU FOREVER."

The term "well-wisher" encapsulates more than a mere lexical definition; it embodies a profound commitment. It transcends linguistic boundaries, evolving beyond a word to symbolize an enduring connection. It represents a silent, unwavering pledge—a promise echoing through time. "Well-wisher" signifies a continuum of support, encapsulating past, present, and future. It is an intricate thread woven into the fabric of relationships, articulating steadfast companionship. In essence, it embodies a timeless devotion, offering solace and encouragement. This phrase encapsulates the depth of commitment and serves as a testament to enduring bonds that persist, transcending the limitations of language.

In a serene village nestled between emerald hills and golden fields, there lived a wise and gentle man named Samuel. He was not just a father to his son, Ethan, but also his confidant and steadfast companion. Samuel believed in the essence of being a well-wisher.

As Ethan grew, Samuel shared tales of his own experiences, imparting wisdom like golden threads weaving through the fabric of their relationship. One evening, under the ancient oak tree near their home, Samuel spoke to Ethan about the profound meaning of being a well-wisher.

"Son," Samuel began, "a well-wisher is more than a word. It's a promise, silent yet resounding. It means being there in every moment—past, present, and future. I was there when your first cries echoed in the air, I am here as we share this moment, and I will be with you forever."

Ethan listened, captivated by his father's words. The sun dipped below the horizon, casting a warm glow on the duo. Samuel continued, "Being a well-wisher means supporting you in your dreams and standing by you in challenges. It's a promise to celebrate your victories and lend a hand in defeat."

As the years unfolded, Samuel and Ethan faced the tapestry of life together. Whether in the joy of achievements or the depths of hardships, the silent promise echoed between them. Samuel's guidance became a beacon, steering Ethan through the stormy seas of adolescence and the uncharted territories of adulthood.

When Samuel's time on this earth drew to a close, Ethan found himself beneath the same ancient oak tree where their conversations had begun. The wind whispered the tales of their shared laughter, struggles, and triumphs. Although Samuel was physically absent, his essence lingered, a testament to the enduring nature of a well-wisher.

Ethan carried his father's teachings, becoming a well-wisher in his own right. In every decision, he heard his father's silent promises echoing, "I was, I am, and I will be with you forever." And so, the legacy of a well-wisher continued, an unbroken chain connecting generations under the watchful branches of the ancient oak tree.

CHAPTER NINETEEN

DAY 19

"YOUR LIFE IS YOUR GARDEN, & YOUR THOUGHTS ARE THE SEEDS. PUT POSITIVE VIBRATION ON YOUR SEEDS FOR CREATION OF POWERFUL ENERGY IN YOUR MIND TO FACE ANY CHALLENGE IN YOUR LIFE."

In the garden of life, your thoughts act as seeds, determining the nature of the energy you cultivate. By sowing positive vibrations, you foster the growth of powerful mental energy. This mindset becomes a resilient force, empowering you to confront and overcome challenges. Just as a well-tended garden thrives, nurturing constructive thoughts yields a flourishing mental landscape. Embracing positivity enhances your capacity to navigate the complexities of life, fostering strength, resilience, and a mindset capable of overcoming any obstacle that comes your way. Cultivate the seeds of optimism, and your inner garden will bloom with the vibrant energy needed to face life's challenges.

In the charming town of Amrithsir, three inseparable friends, Jockson, Noel, and Sharley, stumbled upon the transformative power of positive thinking that would alter the course of their lives. One serene afternoon, they gathered in Sharley's backyard, surrounded by blooming flowers and the gentle rustling of leaves.

Sharley, a free spirit with a deep connection to nature, shared an ancient proverb: "Your life is your garden, and your thoughts are the seeds." Inspired, they decided to embark on a journey to cultivate positivity in their minds.

They began by reflecting on their aspirations, supporting each other's dreams, and collectively banishing negativity. Jockson, the pragmatic thinker, embraced mindfulness techniques, while Noel, the adventurous soul, introduced them to meditation in the serene woods nearby.

As weeks passed, the trio witnessed remarkable changes. Sharley's artistic endeavors flourished, Jockson found innovative solutions at work, and Noel's daring pursuits bore fruit. Their friendship deepened as they navigated life's challenges with newfound resilience.

One day, facing an unexpected setback, they gathered once more, reinforcing their commitment to positive thoughts. Through mutual encouragement, they transformed adversity into an opportunity for growth, reinforcing the idea that the energy they cultivated in their minds could truly shape their destinies.

In the end, the garden of their lives blossomed with vibrant experiences and enduring friendships. Their shared journey underscored the profound truth that by sowing seeds of positivity, they had created a powerful, collective energy capable of overcoming any challenge. As they celebrated their victories under the shade of the same trees where their journey began, the town of Amrithsir echoed with the harmonious laughter of friends who had discovered the transformative magic of nurturing their mental gardens with positivity.

DAY 20

"ACTION IS THE BEST WAY TO BE SUCCESSFUL, BUT IT SHOULD BE CONTINUOUS."

Success is not a one-time event; it thrives on continuous action. The key lies in sustained effort and perseverance. Taking consistent, purposeful steps toward goals builds momentum and fosters growth. Success is not merely achieved through sporadic bursts of action but through a relentless commitment to progress. Each action contributes to a cumulative effect, creating a pathway to achievement. By maintaining a steady pace, challenges become opportunities, failures transform into lessons, and success becomes an enduring journey rather than a destination. In this dynamic process, the commitment to continuous action becomes the cornerstone of lasting success.

In the small town of Perseveranceville, there lived a determined soul named Sushanth. From a young age, Sushanth had a dream of building something extraordinary, something that would leave a lasting impact. Recognizing the value of action, Sushanth embraced the philosophy that consistent effort was the key to success.

Every morning, while the town was still wrapped in the quiet embrace of dawn, Sushanth would set out on a journey of purposeful action. The days turned into weeks, and weeks into months, as Sushanth tirelessly worked on the dream. Challenges arose, obstacles tested resilience, but Sushanth's unwavering commitment to continuous action remained unshaken.

People in Perseveranceville noticed the dedication radiating from Sushanth and began to rally behind the ambitious project. Friends, neighbors, and even skeptics became inspired by the relentless pursuit of success. The town buzzed with a newfound energy, fueled by the belief that progress was possible through consistent, intentional effort.

As seasons changed, so did the landscape of Perseveranceville. The once humble dream started to take shape, growing into a remarkable achievement that surpassed even Sushanth's initial vision. The project became a testament to the transformative power of continuous action.

Through the ups and downs, Sushanth learned that success wasn't a destination but a journey. Each day's work added a layer to the foundation of accomplishment. Failures became stepping stones, and setbacks were viewed as opportunities for growth. The story of Perseveranceville became a beacon of inspiration for neighboring towns, illustrating that success wasn't a stroke of luck but a result of sustained, dedicated effort.

As the years passed, Perseveranceville transformed into a thriving community, and Sushanth, once a dreamer, became a symbol of what could be achieved through unwavering determination. The town's success wasn't a stroke of luck; it was a manifestation of the belief that action, when continuous, could overcome any obstacle.

In the end, Perseveranceville stood as a testament to the simple yet profound truth that action, when coupled with persistence, was the surest path to success. And as the sun set over the town, casting a warm glow on its achievements, the spirit of continuous action echoed through the streets, inspiring generations to come.

CHAPTER TWENTY-ONE

DAY 21

"WORK FOR A CAUSE, NOT FOR APPLAUSE. LIVE LIFE TO EXPRESS, NOT TO IMPRESS. DON'T STRIVE TO MAKE YOUR PRESENCE NOTICED, JUST MAKE YOUR ABSENCE FELT."

Focus on meaningful contributions rather than seeking external validation. Prioritize purposeful work that aligns with your values, emphasizing substance over recognition. Live authentically, expressing yourself genuinely without the need to impress others. Shift your mindset from drawing attention to making a lasting impact. Cultivate a presence that resonates through meaningful actions and positive influence. Let the significance of your absence speak volumes, emphasizing the value you bring. In essence, lead a purpose-driven life that transcends the superficial pursuit of applause, leaving a lasting impression through your meaningful endeavors and the profound impact you make on others and the world.

In the enchanting realm of Mayavana, where ancient hills held the echoes of magical tales and the breeze carried the whispers of secrets, there lived a spirited young girl named Namitha. Her eyes sparkled with the curiosity of the unknown, and her heart resonated with a profound desire to illuminate the shadows that had mysteriously descended upon her mystical homeland.

Mayavana faced an extraordinary challenge—a pervasive darkness that dulled the once-glistening radiance of the magical beings that inhabited the realm. Undeterred by the encroaching shadows, Namitha embarked on a daring journey, armed with a lantern of hope and fueled by an unyielding belief in the transformative power of positive change.

As Namitha ventured into the heart of the enchanted forest, ancient trees whispered tales of old, and mystical creatures emerged to share their ancient wisdom. Guided by an innate connection to the magical energies of Mayavana, Namitha discovered an abandoned temple. Within its forgotten walls, she uncovered a radiant crystal pulsating with untold power.

Cradling the crystal gently, Namitha felt the warmth of its energy course through her being. She understood that this luminous artifact held the key to dispelling the encroaching darkness. With unwavering determination, Namitha returned to Mayavana, facing initial skepticism from her fellow magical beings. Yet, the radiant glow of the crystal and Namitha's steadfast belief gradually won their hearts.

Together, the magical beings united, channeling their collective strength to confront the shadowy presence. Namitha stood at the forefront, holding the crystal high as a beacon of hope, its brilliance casting a powerful glow across Mayavana.

In a climactic confrontation, the darkness recoiled before the crystal's radiant light, revealing its true nature—a manifestation of fear and doubt. As the magical beings embraced unity and courage, the shadows dissipated, and Mayavana was once again bathed in the warm, golden glow of newfound resilience.

Namitha's journey became a timeless legend, passed down through the enchanted realm. Mayavana transformed into a haven of shared purpose, where each magical being, inspired by Namitha's courage, contributed to the well-being of the realm. The luminous crystal, now enshrined in the heart of Mayavana, served as a perpetual reminder that even in the face of adversity, a single individual's determination could ignite a collective flame of positive change.

And so, in the mystical realm of Mayavana, the story of Namitha lived on—a testament to the transformative power of courage, unity, and the unwavering pursuit of a brighter magical tomorrow.

CHAPTER TWENTY-TWO

DAY 22

"IF YOU DON'T AFRAID TO BE FAILURE, YOU WILL SUCCEED DEFINITELY AT THE EARLIEST"

Embracing the absence of fear towards failure cultivates a mindset essential for success. By confronting challenges with courage, individuals can navigate setbacks, learn valuable lessons, and adapt. The absence of fear allows for resilience, perseverance, and a determination to overcome obstacles. Success becomes an inevitable outcome when one views failure not as a deterrent but as a stepping stone towards growth. This mindset encourages innovation, creativity, and a willingness to take calculated risks. Ultimately, those unburdened by the fear of failure embark on a journey marked by continuous improvement and achievement, ensuring success arrives sooner rather than later.

In the lush landscapes of Kerala, where palm trees swayed to the rhythm of gentle winds and the air was infused with the scent of spices, lived a young artist named Ramya. Her heart pulsated with dreams as vast as the tea plantations that adorned the hills. However, an omnipresent fear of failure cast a shadow over her aspirations.

Ramya's days were intertwined with hesitations and self-doubt. The longing to succeed clashed with the apprehension of falling short. It wasn't until an eccentric mentor, a wise old painter named Nagaraj, entered her life that Ramya's perspective began to metamorphose.

On a misty morning, Nagaraj handed Ramya a weathered canvas and an unconventional brush. "To succeed, you must first release your fear of failure," he declared, his eyes radiating wisdom. The brush, he explained, possessed the power to bring dreams to life when wielded without the shackles of fear.

Tentatively, Ramya dipped the brush into vibrant hues, each stroke unraveling a piece of her aspirations. The canvas transformed into a mirror reflecting her journey, a testament to her courage in confronting the blank spaces and imperfections.

As Ramya painted, the people of Kerala observed her transformation. Skepticism lingered, but Ramya persevered, embracing each perceived failure as a stroke adding depth to her narrative. The town, once indifferent, now began to resonate with her evolving perspective.

One day, Ramya's masterpiece caught the eye of a renowned art critic. Enthralled by the raw authenticity of her work, he praised Ramya's ability to translate vulnerability into beauty. The town, initially dubious, now celebrated her as a symbol of resilience.

Ramya's journey became a guiding light for others grappling with their fears. Through her art, she conveyed that success wasn't just about perfection but about the audacity to confront failure and transform it into stepping stones toward growth.

In the end, Ramya discovered that the fear of failure was a canvas waiting to be painted. With every stroke, she redefined success, proving that the truest victories arise not from the absence of fear but from the audacity to confront it. As Kerala basked in the glow of Ramya's triumph, the whispered words of Nagaraj echoed, "If you don't afraid to be failure, you will succeed definitely at the earliest." Ramya had not just painted her dreams; she had painted her liberation from fear, a masterpiece that resonated with the hearts of all who dared to dream in the vibrant landscapes of Kerala.

CHAPTER TWENTY-THREE

DAY 23

"HAPPINESS IS LIKE A PERFUME. YOU CANNOT SPREAD ON OTHERS WITHOUT GETTING FEW DROPS ON YOURSELF. SO ALWAYS BE HAPPY TO MAKE OTHERS HAPPY!"

The analogy "Happiness is like a perfume" suggests that, much like fragrance, happiness has a contagious quality. To spread joy to others, one must first experience it themselves, akin to getting a few drops on one's own skin. This simple yet profound wisdom encourages a positive mindset, emphasizing that personal happiness is essential for creating a ripple effect of joy in the lives of those around us. By cultivating happiness within, individuals contribute to a more harmonious and uplifting social environment. In essence, the quote underscores the interconnectedness of personal well-being and the ability to positively influence others.

In the serene hills of Meghalaya, nestled amidst emerald green landscapes, lived a jovial man named Rakesh. His laughter echoed through the valleys, and his perpetual smile was as refreshing as the mountain breeze. One day, as Rakesh strolled through the quaint village square, he overheard a conversation between two friends, Kishor and Sushanth. They carried the weight of their worries, their faces reflecting the hues of stress and uncertainty.

Feeling a kinship with his fellow villagers, Rakesh decided it was time to share the secret of his radiant joy. "Happiness is like a perfume," he began, his eyes sparkling with the wisdom of the hills. "You can't spread it on others without getting a few drops on yourself. So, always be happy to make others happy."

Intrigued, Kishor and Sushanth listened intently as Rakesh wove a tale of personal joy as the catalyst for a harmonious community. He spoke of the interconnectedness of emotions and the transformative power of positive energy. Rakesh's words resonated, prompting a shift in perspective for his attentive audience.

Inspired by Rakesh's wisdom, Kishor and Sushanth decided to embrace this philosophy. They made a conscious effort to find joy in the simple moments, to relish the beauty of their mountainous surroundings. As their own happiness blossomed, an enchanting transformation occurred in their village. Laughter echoed through the hills, smiles replaced frowns, and the once somber atmosphere gave way to a lively, interconnected community.

Word of Rakesh's wisdom spread like the monsoon rains, reaching the hearts of everyone in Meghalaya. The villagers, in turn, became ambassadors of happiness, creating a positive ripple effect. Rakesh, the inadvertent architect of this joyful transformation, reveled in the realization that his own happiness had become a source of inspiration for an entire community.

As the sun set behind the rolling hills of Meghalaya, it cast a warm glow over a village radiating with happiness.

Rakesh, Kishor, Sushanth, and the entire community embraced the enduring truth that happiness, much like the mountain mists, leaves an indelible trace wherever it touches. The tale of Meghalaya became a testament to the profound impact of personal well-being on the collective spirit of a community in the heart of the Northeastern hills.

CHAPTER TWENTY-FOUR

DAY 24

"WHEN YOU ARE IN THE LIGHT, EVERYTHING FOLLOWS YOU, BUT WHEN YOU ENTER INTO THE DARK, EVEN YOUR OWN SHADOW DOESN'T FOLLOW YOU."

In the light, one's actions and influences are evident, attracting attention and support from others. However, when stepping into darkness, symbolic of challenges or uncertainties, one may experience solitude and lack of support. The notion highlights the transient nature of companionship and success, emphasizing that not all situations elicit unwavering loyalty. It suggests that adversity reveals true allegiances, as even one's shadow, a constant companion in light, may abandon in darkness. Metaphorically, the saying prompts reflection on the dynamic nature of relationships and the importance of resilience when facing life's obscurities.

In the sacred town of Tirupathi, where the divine echoes in every breeze, lived two sisters, Sharadha and Kamala. Their home, nestled against the backdrop of the holy hills, resonated with the serenity of the surroundings. Sharadha, the elder sister, was known for the vibrant rangolis that adorned their doorstep, capturing the essence of the town's spiritual aura. Kamala, younger and more contemplative, found solace in the rhythmic beats of her tabla, a reflection of the divine rhythm that permeated Tirupathi.

Their days were a harmonious blend of Sharadha's artistic flair and Kamala's soulful rhythms, creating a symphony that reverberated through the tranquil town. The sisters, affectionately referred to as the "Divine Duo," brought a unique blend of creativity and spirituality to Tirupathi, enriching the lives of those around them.

Yet, beneath the surface of their serene existence, a subtle tension lingered. Kamala, inspired by the spiritual vibrations of Tirupathi, harbored dreams of exploring her musical talents beyond the sacred hills. She yearned to share her tabla's beats with a broader audience, resonating beyond the temple town's confines.

One auspicious evening, under the sacred canopy of the town's ancient banyan tree, Kamala confided her aspirations to Sharadha. The revelation cast a momentary shadow over the tranquility of their abode. Sharadha, torn between the love for her sister and the fear of disrupting their harmonious life, grappled with conflicting emotions.

As the days unfolded, the sisters navigated this new chapter, learning to embrace the beauty in both light and shadow. Sharadha, recognizing the significance of nurturing individual aspirations, encouraged Kamala to embark on a musical journey while assuring her that their bond would remain unbroken.

Kamala set forth on her musical pilgrimage, her tabla echoing in distant lands, seeking inspiration beyond the holy chants of Tirupathi. Left to create rangolis without her sister's daily presence, Sharadha found a profound depth to her art, capturing not only the spiritual essence of

Tirupathi but also the evolving rhythms of their shared lives.

Seasons changed, and as the sacred hills witnessed the passage of time, Kamala returned to Tirupathi, carrying with her not just musical notes but a deeper understanding of herself. The sisters, reunited, found a richer resonance in their divine harmony. Kamala's experiences had added a new dimension to Sharadha's rangolis, and Sharadha's unwavering support had anchored Kamala's musical explorations.

Tirupathi, observing this evolution, celebrated the Divine Duo anew. The once-pristine canvas of their lives now bore the brushstrokes of growth, resilience, and a shared understanding that light and shadow, when embraced together, create a masterpiece of divine beauty.

And so, Sharadha and Kamala continued to enchant Tirupathi, not just with the vibrant colors of rangolis or the melodious beats of the tabla but with the profound harmony born from their individual journeys—a testament to the enduring strength of sisterhood in the sacred embrace of Tirupathi's hills.

CHAPTER TWENTY-FIVE

DAY 25

"Hurting someone is as easy as like plucking a leaf from Tree. But getting someone's trust, is like growing a tree. It takes lot of Time, Care & Patience."

Inflicting harm upon someone can be effortless, akin to plucking a leaf from a tree, a swift action with immediate impact. Conversely, gaining someone's trust is a gradual, intricate process reminiscent of nurturing a tree. It demands considerable time, careful attention, and unwavering patience. Just as a tree grows over the seasons, trust flourishes with consistent efforts and genuine intentions. The fragility of trust underscores the need for delicate cultivation, emphasizing the stark contrast between the simplicity of causing harm and the complexity of building a foundation rooted in trust, which stands resilient like a well-nurtured tree over time.

In the vibrant city of Chennai, where the warm sea breeze carried the scent of spices and the streets echoed with the rhythm of Carnatic music, lived a couple named Raju and Pavitra. Their love story unfolded against the backdrop of bustling markets and traditional dance performances.

Raju, an enterprising entrepreneur navigating the dynamic business landscape, crossed paths with Pavitra, a strategic business consultant with a flair for innovation. Their connection ignited, resonating with the harmony of their shared dreams.

Over aromatic dinners in the city's bustling neighborhoods and strategic discussions in coffee-scented meeting rooms, their love deepened, creating a narrative woven with the threads of professional and personal achievements.

One day, Raju surprised Pavitra with a thoughtfully planned business venture, a testament to their shared entrepreneurial spirit. In turn, Pavitra orchestrated a strategic marketing campaign that propelled Raju's latest project to new heights. Chennai became the canvas for their shared triumphs and the stage where they performed the dance of their dreams.

Yet, as in any business venture, challenges emerged. A disagreement, like a temporary monsoon shower, tested their partnership. Instead of letting it escalate, Raju and Pavitra chose open communication, nurturing the roots of their relationship. It was a demonstration of resilience, much like the thriving businesses lining Chennai's streets.

As the years passed, so did their love, evolving into a partnership that withstood market dynamics and embraced both successes and setbacks. Together, they navigated the business landscape of Chennai, their shared visions and strategic planning forming a love story as enduring as the rich cultural tapestry of the city.

CHAPTER TWENTY-SIX

DAY 26

"SMALL & SIMPLE FORMULA FOR A BETTER LIFE: DON'T LOOK FOR THE PERSON WHO WILL SOLVE ALL YOUR PROBLEMS. BUT LOOK FOR THE PERSON WHO WILL BE WITH YOU IN ALL YOUR PROBLEMS."

In the pursuit of a better life, the essence lies in choosing companionship over problem-solving prowess. Rather than seeking someone to miraculously solve every woe, the key is to find a person who stands steadfast beside you through thick and thin. This small yet profound formula underscores the importance of emotional support and shared resilience in navigating life's challenges. It promotes the idea that enduring connections and shared burdens contribute more significantly to well-being than the fleeting relief of having someone solve individual problems. It's a call to prioritize relationships built on enduring solidarity for a more fulfilling life journey.

Once upon a time in a quaint town nestled between rolling hills and babbling brooks, there lived a curious young girl named Sunitha. Known for her insatiable thirst for knowledge, Sunitha spent her days exploring the hidden corners of the town, discovering its secrets.

One brisk autumn day, as golden leaves carpeted the cobblestone streets, Sunitha stumbled upon an ancient bookstore tucked away in a forgotten alley. Intrigued, she pushed open the creaking door to find a cozy haven of books, each whispering tales of distant lands and forgotten times.

The elderly bookstore owner, Mr. Kiran, welcomed Sunitha with a warm smile. Sensing her love for stories, he handed her a dusty leather-bound book. Its pages seemed to hold the magic of centuries, and as Sunitha flipped through, a shimmering light enveloped her.

Transported into a fantastical realm, Sunitha found herself in a bustling city of floating lanterns and talking animals. The book had woven a portal to a land where dreams and reality danced together. With wide-eyed wonder, Sunitha embarked on an adventure, meeting characters straight from the pages of classic tales.

As Sunitha traversed enchanted forests and crossed rivers of liquid silver, she encountered challenges that mirrored those in her own life. The wise old owl taught her the value of patience, and the mischievous pixie showed her the joy of embracing spontaneity. Through these lessons, Sunitha began to understand that the true magic lay not in escaping problems but in facing them with newfound strength.

Days turned into nights, and Sunitha's journey became a tapestry of courage, friendship, and self-discovery. The characters she met became steadfast companions, teaching her that life's challenges were but chapters in a grand narrative.

Eventually, Sunitha stumbled upon a portal back to the quaint town. Grateful for the magical journey, she returned to Mr. Kiran's bookstore, where time seemed to stand still. With a twinkle in his eye, Mr. Kiran explained that the book chose its readers wisely, opening doors to worlds where one could find not only answers but also the resilience to face life's uncertainties.

As Sunitha stepped back into her familiar surroundings, she carried the stories within her, forever grateful for the simple yet profound truth: Life's magic lies not in escaping problems but in embracing the journey and the companions who walk beside us through it all. And so, in that quaint town between the hills and brooks, Sunitha continued her adventures, knowing that each chapter, whether ordinary or extraordinary, added richness to the grand story of her life.

DAY 27

"LIFE IS THE MOST DIFFICULT EXAM. MANY PEOPLE FAIL BECAUSE THEY TRY TO COPY OTHERS, NOT REALIZING THAT EVERYONE HAS A DIFFERENT QUESTION PAPER."

Life is an intricate exam, and many stumble by imitating others, oblivious to the fact that each person confronts a unique set of challenges. The metaphor underscores the individuality of human experiences, emphasizing that there's no universal roadmap to success or fulfillment. Mimicking someone else's path may not align with one's inherent strengths or circumstances. To triumph in life's exam, authenticity and self-awareness are paramount. Recognizing the distinctiveness of personal challenges and forging a path aligned with one's true self fosters resilience and the ability to navigate the unpredictable terrain of existence. Embrace your individual question paper; it holds the key to your own triumphs.

In the bustling town of Kalipong, a diverse tapestry of lives unfolded. Among its inhabitants were Jeff and Noel, two young dreamers navigating the maze of life. As the saying went, "Life is the most difficult exam. Many people fail because they try to copy others, not realizing that everyone has a different question paper."

Jeff and Noel, enthralled by the success stories of friends and celebrities, yearned to replicate their journeys. Day by day, the pursuit of imitation left them disoriented and unfulfilled. It became evident that the borrowed paths weren't aligned with their personal passions and strengths.

One fateful day, a chance encounter with an old artist named Clara shifted Jeff and Noel's perspective. Clara, with her vibrant strokes of wisdom, shared, "Life's exam isn't about imitating others. It's about understanding your unique question paper." Inspired, Jeff and Noel embarked on a journey of self-discovery, embracing individuality.

With newfound authenticity, Jeff and Noel faced life's challenges head-on. The journey was still demanding, but resilience grew from an unwavering connection to personal values. As time unfolded, their story became a testament to the power of authenticity.

Kalipong, with its varied inhabitants, echoed the truth that success wasn't universal. Each person's question paper bore distinct challenges and opportunities. Embracing this diversity, the town thrived as individuals like Jeff and Noel discovered their authentic paths, realizing that copying others only led to a hollow victory.

In the end, Jeff and Noel's story resonated not just in Kalipong but beyond, a reminder that life's true triumph lay in navigating the unique terrain of one's own question paper.

CHAPTER TWENTY-EIGHT

DAY 28

"NEVER DESIGN YOUR CHARACTER LIKE A GARDEN WHERE ANYONE CAN WALK. DESIGN YOUR CHARACTER LIKE THE SKY WHERE EVERYONE DESIRES TO REACH."

Craft your character like an elusive sky, not an accessible garden. Gardens invite all to stroll, their charm diluted by common footsteps. In contrast, the sky, vast and ethereal, beckons admiration and aspiration. Its heights elicit longing, a realm coveted by all. Similarly, when constructing your character, evoke a sense of awe and yearning. Be a figure others aspire to emulate, a beacon of inspiration in the limitless expanse of human potential. Let your essence soar high, a celestial force that captivates hearts and fuels the collective desire to ascend beyond ordinary realms.

In the quaint village of Provence, France, where the aroma of lavender wafted through the air and the cobblestone streets told tales of centuries gone by, three friends embarked on a journey that would forever intertwine their destinies.

Alex, with his unruly curls and a heart as vast as the vineyards surrounding the village, was a painter seeking inspiration. Kamal, a spirited soul with roots in Morocco, was a chef eager to infuse the flavors of his heritage into French cuisine. Naveed, the quiet philosopher among them, found solace in the vineyards, contemplating the essence of life amid rows of grapevines.

One fateful summer, the trio decided to renovate an abandoned chateau on the outskirts of the village. The dilapidated walls echoed with the whispers of the past, inspiring Alex's art and providing a canvas for his vibrant strokes. Kamal, in the heart of the village, discovered a small, neglected bistro that would become the stage for his culinary masterpieces, blending the richness of Morocco with the elegance of French gastronomy.

As they immersed themselves in their pursuits, the village embraced the trio's endeavors, weaving a tapestry of cultural fusion. Locals and tourists alike flocked to the chateau-cum-gallery, where Alex's paintings adorned the walls like portals to different dimensions. Kamal's bistro, named "Saffron Skies," became renowned for its eclectic menu, a testament to the diversity of friendship and flavor.

Naveed, while nurturing the vineyards, discovered the art of winemaking, blending the traditions of the French countryside with a touch of his philosophical musings. The chateau's cellars bore witness to the alchemy of his creations, each bottle telling a story of friendship, passion, and the union of diverse worlds.

Through the seasons, the trio's bond deepened, and their individual crafts flourished. The village, once a backdrop, became a character in their narrative—a silent supporter applauding their triumphs and comforting them in moments of doubt.

As the sun dipped below the horizon on the first anniversary of their venture, the village square hosted a celebration, echoing with laughter, clinking glasses, and the harmonious blend of French and Arabic melodies. The trio, standing side by side, gazed at the chateau now bathed in the warm glow of lanterns, a testament to their shared dreams.

In that moment, as the stars emerged in the Provencal sky, Alex, Kamal, and Naveed realized that their story was not just a tale of individual pursuits but a symphony of friendship that resonated far beyond the borders of their adopted village—a harmonious melody in the heart of France, where cultures collided, dreams soared, and the essence of life was savored like a fine wine.

CHAPTER TWENTY-NINE

DAY 29

"MEMORIES ARE ALWAYS SPECIAL, SOMETIMES. WE LAUGH BY REMEMBERING THE DAYS WE CRIED. AND SOMETIMES WE CRY BY REMEMBERING THE DAYS WE LAUGHED."

Memories carry a profound duality, shaping our emotional landscape. In their special tapestry, laughter and tears are interwoven threads. The recollection of past sorrows can unexpectedly elicit present joy, revealing the resilience in overcoming challenges. Conversely, reminiscing about days filled with laughter may evoke tears, underscoring the complex nature of human experience. These contrasting emotions encapsulate the richness of our journey, reminding us that each memory holds the power to evoke laughter, tears, or both. Ultimately, it is this emotional mosaic that paints the canvas of our lives, making every memory a poignant and cherished chapter in our personal narrative.

In the heart of Nagaland, amid mist-covered hills and vibrant valleys, lived an inquisitive girl named Raksha. Aged ten, Raksha stumbled upon an ancient, dust-laden tome in her grandfather's attic. Its pages whispered of a forgotten magical realm concealed beyond the veils of reality. Drawn by an irresistible curiosity, Raksha embarked on an extraordinary journey.

Guided by the iridescent glow of fireflies one starry night, Raksha discovered the entrance to the mystical realm. Stepping through, she entered a world where trees sang enchanting melodies, and the air shimmered with ancient magic. Raksha befriended talking animals and encountered mythical creatures, unraveling the realm's secrets.

Delving deeper, Raksha uncovered a neglected prophecy foretelling the realm's fading magic. Only a child with a pure heart could rekindle its enchantment. Understanding her destiny, Raksha embarked on a quest, facing challenges testing her courage and compassion.

On her journey, Raksha encountered a mischievous sprite, a venerable wizard, and a lonely dragon. Each became a trusted ally, contributing their unique abilities to aid her quest. Together, they traversed enchanted forests, crossed perilous rivers, and climbed towering mountains.

The climax unfolded in the heart of the realm, where a mystical fountain held the key to restoring magic. Yet, a formidable guardian protected it. Raksha faced the ultimate test, drawing upon lessons learned from her companions and the challenges overcome.

With unwavering determination, Raksha triumphed over adversity. As she touched the fountain, magic surged through the realm. Colors brightened, flowers danced, and the once-silent breeze whispered gratitude. The prophecy fulfilled, Raksha bid farewell to her newfound friends, returning to Nagaland.

As Raksha stepped back through the portal, the ancient book in her hand began to glow. She realized her adventure wasn't merely a tale; it was a cherished gift passed through generations. Inspired, Raksha preserved the story, ensuring the magic of her extraordinary journey would endure, bringing enchantment to future generations in Nagaland. And so, the legacy of Raksha's magical adventure lived on, weaving into the rich tapestry of Nagaland's folklore.

CHAPTER THIRTY

DAY 30

"PATIENCE IS NOT ABOUT THE ABILITY TO WAIT, BUT THE ABILITY TO KEEP A GOOD ATTITUDE WHILE WAITING."

Patience transcends mere waiting; it entails maintaining a positive attitude during the passage of time. It's a virtue characterized by resilience and composure in the face of delays or uncertainties. Rather than passively enduring, true patience involves an active choice to remain optimistic and focused on the eventual outcome. Cultivating patience nurtures emotional resilience, fostering a mindset capable of navigating challenges with grace. This mental fortitude not only enhances personal well-being but also strengthens interpersonal relationships and problem-solving skills. Ultimately, patience is a powerful tool for personal growth, promoting a sense of calm and perspective in the midst of life's uncertainties.

In the quaint town of Ooty, where cobblestone streets whispered tales of time, lived an elderly woman named Simitha. At 85, she was a reservoir of stories, her eyes reflecting the kaleidoscope of experiences she'd collected over the years. Yet, her most cherished tale remained untold.

Every evening, Simitha would sit on her porch, knitting needles clacking like a secret code. The townsfolk, curious and enchanted, wondered about the elusive story hidden within the wrinkles of her smile. One autumn evening, a curious young girl named Sindhya Balan approached Simitha, her eyes brimming with wonder.

"Simitha," Sindhya Balan implored, "what's the story behind that gleam in your eyes?"

Simitha chuckled, inviting Sindhya Balan to sit. With the setting sun casting a warm glow, she began her tale. It unfolded like a cherished heirloom, each word a thread weaving the fabric of time.

Simitha's story started in her youth when Ooty was a canvas painted in vibrant hues. She spoke of love found and lost, dreams chased and reshaped. But the heart of her narrative lay in a promise made under the ancient oak tree, where she vowed to wait for her true love, Jain.

As the years passed, Simitha's eyes sparkled with the reflection of memories. She spoke of the bittersweet symphony of waiting—seasons changing, leaves falling, and the passage of time etching lines on her hands. Jain, a soldier, had promised to return, and Simitha faithfully waited, knitting the fabric of her life with hope.

The townsfolk, captivated by Simitha's narrative, felt the weight of her patience. Ooty became a haven of empathy, neighbors sharing their own stories of resilience. As seasons changed and the oak tree witnessed the ebb and flow of life, Simitha's tale became a beacon of endurance and love.

One crisp morning, when the first snowflakes adorned Ooty, a stranger approached. A weathered man, his eyes mirrored Simitha's. It was Jain, returning after decades, fulfilling the promise made beneath the ancient oak. The town rejoiced in the reunion, a testament to the enduring power of patience.

Simitha's porch, once a seat for solitude, now hosted laughter and warmth. The town of Ooty, inspired by her unwavering patience, discovered that every story, no matter how delayed, had its perfect moment to unfold. And so, Ooty continued to be a town where time painted its stories on cobblestone streets, and the echo of patience resonated through the years.

CHAPTER THIRTY-ONE

DAY 31

"THE SEA IS THE SAME FOR ALL BUT SOME FIND FISHES, SOME FIND SHELLS, SOME FIND PEARLS & OTHERS JUST WET THEIR FEET. LIFE IS THE SAME FOR ALL, WE ONLY FIND WHAT WE ARE LOOKING FOR. CHOOSE WISELY."

In life's vast sea, each person navigates unique waters. Some diligently search, uncovering treasures like shimmering pearls, while others contentedly collect shells. Some dive deep for the elusive fish, driven by ambition. Then there are those who merely dip their toes, savoring the simple joys. The sea remains constant, indifferent to the varied pursuits. Likewise, life unfolds universally, offering diverse opportunities. What one discovers depends on the chosen perspective and pursuit. It is a reminder that life's richness lies not just in the vastness of the sea but in the intent with which one explores, encouraging us to choose our quests wisely.

Once upon a time in a small coastal village, there lived a curious young girl named Leena. Every morning, as the sun painted the sky in hues of pink and gold, Leena would venture to the beach, her favorite place in the world.

One day, as she strolled along the shore, a mysterious bottle caught her eye. Intrigued, Leena picked it up and discovered a weathered piece of parchment inside. Unfurling the ancient note, she read about a legendary underwater realm where wishes came true. The catch? Only those with pure hearts could find it.

Determined, Leena set off on a quest to unlock the secrets of this enchanted realm. Guided by the whispers of the ocean, she faced challenges that tested her kindness and courage. Along the way, Leena made unlikely friends—a wise old turtle and a playful dolphin—who became her companions.

As Leena delved deeper into the unknown, she encountered a mystical gateway beneath the waves. The moment she crossed it, she found herself in a breathtaking city of coral and pearls. The underwater world shimmered with magic, and Leena felt a profound connection to the sea.

In the heart of the realm, Leena met the Ocean Queen, a regal figure with eyes that held the wisdom of the ages. The Queen explained that Leena's pure heart had led her to this extraordinary place. Grateful for Leena's kindness, the Queen granted her a single wish.

With humility and grace, Leena made her wish—not for riches or power, but for the well-being of her village and the sea that had become her second home. As she emerged from the depths, Leena discovered that her village prospered, and the once-threatened marine life flourished.

Word of Leena's journey spread, inspiring others to approach life with open hearts. The coastal village transformed into a haven of compassion and unity, echoing the magic Leena had found beneath the waves.

From that day forward, every sunrise painted the sky with hues of hope and gratitude, as the once-simple village embraced the profound truth that the most extraordinary discoveries often begin with a pure heart and a curious spirit like Leena's.

CHAPTER THIRTY-TWO

DAY 32

"EVERYTHING IS WITHIN YOUR POWER, AND YOUR POWER IS WITHIN YOU."

This empowering statement emphasizes self-empowerment and the intrinsic ability within individuals to shape their destinies. It encapsulates the idea that one possesses the capacity to control and influence their circumstances. By recognizing and harnessing internal strengths and resources, individuals can overcome challenges and pursue their goals. The phrase encourages self-belief, resilience, and a positive mindset, implying that the potential for achievement lies within one's own capabilities. It serves as a motivational reminder that empowerment originates from within, fostering a sense of confidence and determination to navigate life's journey with a proactive and optimistic perspective.

In the breathtaking region of Kashmir, where majestic mountains cradle serene valleys, there lived a young girl named Keerthi. Today marked a significant day for her — her 1-year birthday. In this land steeped in folklore and mystique, Keerthi shared a special bond with an ancient Chinar tree in her backyard.

According to local legend, this tree possessed magical properties, granting a single wish to those who held steadfast belief in its enchantment. Keerthi, an imaginative soul, had visited the tree since she could toddle. As she approached it on her birthday, the dappled sunlight filtering through its leaves seemed to dance in celebration.

With a heart full of sincerity, Keerthi closed her eyes and whispered her heartfelt wish. To her surprise, a gentle breeze enveloped her, and the Chinar tree's leaves rustled in approval. Unbeknownst to her, the wish had set in motion a series of events that would change the course of Keerthi's life.

The following morning, Keerthi awoke to find a mysterious, ornate key on her bedside table. Intrigued, she followed an invisible thread of destiny, leading her to a forgotten door at the base of the magical Chinar tree. With trepidation and excitement, Keerthi turned the key in the lock, and the door creaked open to reveal a fantastical world beyond.

It was a realm of talking animals, vibrant landscapes, and swirling colors. Keerthi, now the protagonist of her own adventure, embarked on a journey of self-discovery and courage. Along the way, she encountered challenges that tested her resolve, made friends with whimsical creatures, and discovered the depths of her own capabilities.

As the days unfolded, Keerthi's perspective on life expanded, and her connection with the magical Chinar tree deepened. She learned that the true magic lay not only in wishes granted but in the journey itself. On her return to the enchanting land of Kashmir, Keerthi carried the lessons of the enchanted realm, sharing stories of resilience, friendship, and the boundless potential within.

The people of Kashmir, initially skeptical, began to embrace the magic in Keerthi's tales, realizing that belief and courage could open doors to extraordinary possibilities. And so, the legend of Keerthi and the magical Chinar tree became an enduring part of Kashmir's folklore, inspiring generations to come to believe in the power within and the enchantment that awaited those willing to seek it.

CHAPTER THIRTY-THREE

DAY 33

"LIFE IS A PUZZLE WITH DIFFICULTIES, WE HAVE TO SOLVE IT TO GET THE BEST."

Life presents itself as a complex puzzle, brimming with challenges and intricacies. Navigating this intricate maze requires problem-solving skills and resilience. Each challenge encountered contributes a piece to the puzzle, demanding thoughtful consideration and strategic solutions. Success emerges not merely from avoiding difficulties but actively engaging with them. The journey of life becomes a continuous process of deciphering, adapting, and overcoming obstacles. By embracing these challenges, individuals unlock personal growth and uncover the hidden gems within the puzzle of existence. The pursuit of the best outcomes lies not in evasion but in confronting and solving the puzzles that life unfolds.

Rahul and Siri, a couple with a zest for adventure, found themselves lost in the heart of Nalamala Forest during their hiking expedition. The towering trees and dense foliage obscured any semblance of direction, and the couple soon realized they were ensnared in nature's labyrinth.

As dusk settled and the forest echoed with mysterious sounds, Rahul and Siri knew they had to confront the challenge before them. They took a deep breath, reminding each other that life itself was a puzzle to be solved. Armed with this mindset, they began their journey to escape the green maze that surrounded them.

The first hurdle appeared in the form of tangled vines, blocking their path. With teamwork and perseverance, they unraveled the vines, metaphorically untangling the complexities of their situation. The couple realized that life, like the forest, often presented intricate challenges that required collaboration and determination.

As they ventured deeper, a sudden downpour transformed the forest floor into a muddy obstacle course. Every step became a test of balance and adaptability. Rahul and Siri laughed amidst the raindrops, understanding that life's difficulties could be weathered with a positive outlook and a willingness to embrace the unexpected.

Nightfall brought another challenge—a dense fog that shrouded their surroundings. The couple faced moments of uncertainty and fear, mirroring the ambiguity of life's journey. Yet, guided by the faint stars above, they pressed on, understanding that clarity often emerged from navigating through life's foggy moments.

Rahul and Siri's perseverance led them to a raging river, a formidable barrier blocking their way. Life, like the river, sometimes demanded courage to forge ahead. They fashioned a makeshift raft from fallen branches and, with grit and determination, navigated the swift currents, emerging on the other side stronger and more resilient.

Days turned into nights, and their journey through Nalamala Forest began to mirror the twists and turns of life itself. Yet, guided by the belief that every challenge was an opportunity, Rahul and Siri embraced each difficulty. The forest, initially a daunting puzzle, became a metaphor for life's intricate journey.

Finally, a clearing emerged, and sunlight filtered through the trees. Rahul and Siri stepped into an open expanse, victorious in their escape. Nalamala Forest, once a maze of difficulties, had become a transformative experience. They understood that life's puzzles, no matter how daunting, could be unraveled with perseverance, adaptability, and a shared sense of purpose.

As they emerged from Nalamala Forest, Rahul and Siri looked back, grateful for the lessons learned. Life, they realized, was indeed a puzzle with difficulties, but it was through overcoming these challenges that they discovered the best within themselves and each other. Nalamala Forest, now behind them, served as a poignant reminder that every puzzle solved was a step closer to embracing the richness of life's journey.

CHAPTER THIRTY-FOUR

DAY 34

"NO ONE IN THIS WORLD IS PURE AND PERFECT. IF YOU AVOID PEOPLE FOR THEIR MISTAKES, YOU WILL BE ALONE IN THIS WORLD. SO JUDGE LESS AND LOVE MORE."

This quote emphasizes the imperfection inherent in humanity, urging a compassionate perspective. It asserts that perfection is unattainable, and isolating oneself due to others' mistakes leads to loneliness. The message encourages tolerance, advocating for less judgment and more love. By acknowledging the fallibility of individuals and embracing their flaws, one can foster connection and understanding in a world where everyone grapples with imperfections. It serves as a reminder to prioritize empathy over criticism, recognizing the shared humanity that binds us all and promoting a more compassionate and inclusive approach to interpersonal relationships.

In the quiet hum of their shared space, Ishani and Michael navigated the intricate dance of marriage. They had weathered storms and reveled in sunshine, their bond an evolving testament to the ebb and flow of life.

One evening, the air between them hung heavy with unspoken tension. Ishani, meticulously folding laundry, stole glances at Michael absorbed in his work. Unspoken grievances lingered in the room like ghosts, threatening the delicate equilibrium they had built.

As the silence grew, Ishani took a deep breath, breaking the invisible barrier. "Michael," she began tentatively, "I've noticed we've been more critical of each other lately. Small things seem to magnify into mountains."

Michael looked up, his gaze meeting hers with a mixture of acknowledgment and apprehension. The room brimmed with unsaid words until Ishani, echoing the wisdom of ages, uttered, "No one in this world is pure and perfect. If we avoid each other for our mistakes, we'll be alone in this world. Let's judge less and love more."

Those words hung in the air, a profound reminder of their shared humanity. Michael softened, the weight of unspoken grievances lifting. In the vulnerability of the moment, they admitted to their imperfections, embracing the messy beauty of their flawed selves.

From that evening forward, a subtle shift occurred in their relationship. Instead of dwelling on shortcomings, they chose understanding. Mistakes became opportunities for growth, and forgiveness flowed as a healing balm. The realization that perfection was an unattainable mirage allowed them to forge a deeper connection based on acceptance and love.

Days turned into weeks, and the couple found joy in rediscovering the nuances of each other's quirks. Laughter returned, infused with a newfound appreciation for the uniqueness they brought to the union. Through their commitment to judge less and love more, Ishani and Michael discovered that imperfections could be the threads that wove a richer, more resilient tapestry of marriage.

In the quiet hum of their shared space, the echoes of "No one in this world is pure and perfect" lingered, a guiding mantra that transformed their relationship into a sanctuary of acceptance and enduring love.

CHAPTER THIRTY-FIVE

DAY 35

"DON'T TALK, JUST ACT. DON'T SAY, JUST SHOW. DON'T PROMISE, JUST PROVE."

This quote emphasizes the power of action over words, urging individuals to demonstrate their intentions through deeds rather than mere promises. It advocates for a proactive approach to life, where actions speak louder than verbal assurances. By prioritizing tangible results over verbal commitments, it encourages authenticity and credibility. The essence lies in the transformative impact of taking initiative and showcasing one's capabilities through concrete actions, fostering a culture of reliability and accountability. In essence, it promotes a philosophy of substance and achievement, challenging individuals to substantiate their claims with real-world evidence and accomplishments.

In the vibrant city of Hyderabad, two friends, Arya and Ajay, embarked on a journey to overcome life's hurdles, guided by a mantra etched in their hearts: "Don't talk, just act. Don't say, just show. Don't promise, just prove."

Arya, an impassioned artist, aspired to showcase her creations on a global stage. Meanwhile, Ajay, a pragmatic engineer, aimed to revolutionize renewable energy. Their dreams faced formidable challenges, but their friendship provided unwavering support.

Amidst the bustling streets of Hyderabad, Arya's art struggled for recognition, drowned in a sea of conformity. Ajay encountered setbacks in implementing his green energy solutions, hindered by bureaucratic obstacles. However, the duo refused to be disheartened, turning their shared philosophy into a beacon of motivation.

Arya poured her soul into creating breathtaking masterpieces, determined to make her mark. Ajay, undeterred, focused on refining his innovative ideas and tirelessly advocated for change. Their actions became a testament to the resilience encapsulated in their mantra.

In the heart of Hyderabad, Arya's art exhibitions mesmerized audiences, painting tales of resilience with vibrant strokes. Ajay's green energy initiatives gained momentum, transforming the city into a model of sustainable living. Together, they proved that actions spoke louder than setbacks.

As challenges persisted, Arya and Ajay found solace in each other's unwavering determination. Late nights were filled with laughter, tears, and encouragement, embodying the essence of their shared philosophy. They transformed adversity into stepping stones towards success.

Arya's art garnered international acclaim, while Ajay's breakthrough in sustainable energy solutions earned him accolades. Hyderabad, once a backdrop for their struggles, now stood as a testament to their shared journey, inspiring others to turn aspirations into realities.

In the bustling streets of Hyderabad, a mural painted by Arya captured the essence of their triumph — two friends facing storms hand in hand, proving that dreams aren't fulfilled through words alone. The mantra that guided them echoed through the city, inspiring a generation to turn aspirations into realities: "Don't talk, just act. Don't say, just show. Don't promise, just prove."

CHAPTER THIRTY-SIX

DAY 36

"OUR LIFE IS A CREATION OF OUR MIND. EXPECT NOTHING & ACCEPT EVERYTHING. DON'T BELIEVE IN 'TIT FOR TAT' RULE. LEARN TO "LET GO". BECAUSE WE CAN'T EVEN HAVE THE NEXT BREATH UNTIL WE LET GO THE EXISTING ONE!!!"

Our life is shaped by our mindset. Adopting a mindset of expecting nothing and embracing everything promotes resilience. Rejecting the notion of a 'tit for tat' mentality encourages a generous and forgiving outlook. Learning to "let go" is emphasized, underscoring the importance of releasing the past to make room for the present and future. The analogy of releasing a breath underscores the imperative of relinquishing the old to welcome the new. This philosophy advocates mental flexibility, resilience, and a harmonious approach to life, urging individuals to navigate challenges with an open mind and a spirit of acceptance.

In the heart of a bustling city, where the rhythm of life often echoed with hurried footsteps and ambitious dreams, there lived a man named Prabhakar. He was an architect by profession, crafting buildings that touched the sky. Yet, within the edifices of his success, Prabhakar discovered a void that yearned for fulfillment.

One day, as he perched on the rooftop of his latest creation, he reflected on the philosophy that life is a creation of the mind. This notion, filled with the promise of profound change, tugged at the corners of Prabhakar's consciousness. Inspired, he decided to embark on a journey of self-discovery, embracing the idea of expecting nothing and accepting everything.

In the architectural world, the 'tit for tat' rule often dictated exchanges. However, Prabhakar chose a different path. He started a project aimed at creating affordable housing for the less fortunate, defying the conventional norms of reciprocity. His peers raised eyebrows, but Prabhakar found joy in giving without expecting anything in return.

As the construction progressed, Prabhakar faced challenges. The city's bureaucracy resisted change, and critics doubted the viability of his altruistic endeavor. In those moments, he reminded himself to 'let go' of control and trust the process. Every setback became an opportunity to practice the art of releasing attachments.

Months passed, and the housing project transformed into a symbol of resilience. Prabhakar's mindset, rooted in the belief that life was a canvas waiting to be painted, resonated with those who witnessed his journey. The community rallied behind him, breaking the shackles of skepticism and embracing the spirit of collaboration.

Upon completion, the affordable housing complex stood tall, a testament to Prabhakar's unwavering belief in the power of the mind. The lives it touched were not just sheltered but inspired to pay forward the kindness they received. Prabhakar, having sown seeds of change, marveled at the vibrant garden of human connection that blossomed in the wake of his unconventional venture.

In the twilight of his career, Prabhakar found a sense of fulfillment that transcended the blueprints he drafted. He realized that the true masterpiece was not just in the structures he built but in the lives he touched through a mind that expected nothing, accepted everything, rejected the 'tit for tat' rule, and mastered the art of letting go. And as he took a deep breath atop his creation, Prabhakar reveled in the truth that to have the next breath, one must gracefully release the existing one.

CHAPTER THIRTY-SEVEN

DAY 37

"YOUR DIRECTION IS MORE IMPORTANT THAN YOUR SPEED."

In the journey of life, the emphasis on direction surpasses the significance of speed. While swift progress may seem appealing, the ultimate destination and purpose hold greater value. A thoughtful and purposeful direction ensures meaningful accomplishments, fostering personal growth and fulfillment. Speed alone may lead to hasty decisions and missed opportunities. By prioritizing direction, individuals can navigate challenges with intention, learning valuable lessons along the way. It underscores the importance of strategic planning, deliberate choices, and a clear vision, allowing one to achieve enduring success rather than mere rapid advancement. In essence, the right path yields lasting rewards beyond the allure of quick pace.

Bindhu found herself standing at the crossroads of life, torn between the allure of rapid progress and the wisdom of a deliberate journey. Fueled by ambition, she had always raced towards success, often neglecting the significance of direction. One day, exhausted and disoriented, she stumbled upon an old bookstore.

In the quiet haven of dusty shelves, a wise old librarian shared a simple truth: "Your direction is more important than your speed." Intrigued, Bindhu pondered this revelation. She decided to pause, reassess, and chart a purposeful course.

As the seasons changed, so did Bindhu. She embraced the art of mindfulness, making intentional choices that aligned with her values. The world seemed to slow down, revealing hidden treasures in the moments she had overlooked in her haste.

Bindhu's newfound direction led her to unexpected opportunities. She formed meaningful connections, cultivated a sense of inner peace, and discovered passions buried beneath the surface. The pursuit of a deliberate path not only enhanced her personal journey but also rippled positively into the lives of those around her.

In the end, Bindhu realized that life was not a sprint but a mosaic of experiences. The wisdom of choosing the right path over speed transformed her into a beacon of inspiration for others navigating their own crossroads. As she continued her journey, guided by purpose, Bindhu understood that the true essence of success lay not in the swiftness of the journey but in the richness of the direction chosen.

CHAPTER THIRTY-EIGHT

DAY 38

"PLAN WELL BEFORE U START THE JOURNEY IN EVERY WALK OF LIFE. REMEMBER THE CARPENTER AND TAILOR'S RULES... MEASURE TWICE, BUT CUT ONCE."

"Prioritize meticulous planning before embarking on life's diverse journeys. Adhere to the timeless wisdom of carpenters and tailors: 'Measure twice, but cut once.' This mantra underscores the importance of careful consideration and precision in decision-making. Whether shaping a career, relationships, or personal growth, the principle remains steadfast. Each step in life's tapestry demands thoughtful measurement and strategic foresight. Embrace the discipline of measured actions to mitigate risks and enhance outcomes. The analogy of the carpenter and tailor serves as a guiding beacon, urging individuals to be deliberate, ensuring that choices are well-calibrated before executing them in the grand mosaic of existence."

Once upon a time in the picturesque town of Shimla, nestled amidst the snow-capped mountains and pine-scented air, there lived a curious young girl named Naziya. Today marked a special occasion—it was Naziya's twelfth birthday, and the townsfolk had gathered to celebrate in the town square adorned with colorful banners and fragrant flowers.

Naziya's eyes sparkled with excitement as she received a mysterious package from the eccentric old woman, Shakuntala, who dwelled on the outskirts of Shimla. The package contained an ancient-looking map, its edges frayed with age, leading to the fabled Enchanted Grove hidden deep within the mystical Mistwood Forest.

Undeterred by the ominous stories surrounding Mistwood, Naziya decided to embark on an extraordinary journey, fueled by curiosity and the thrill of adventure. Armed with the map and her trusty lantern, she ventured into the heart of Mistwood, where the trees whispered secrets and ethereal lights danced in the air.

As Naziya navigated the labyrinthine paths, she encountered magical creatures that shared tales of an ancient prophecy foretelling the arrival of a brave soul who would unlock the Grove's hidden wonders. The forest seemed to come alive with each step, revealing breathtaking landscapes and enchanting melodies that resonated in harmony with Naziya's heartbeat.

Guided by the map's cryptic symbols, Naziya finally reached the entrance to the Enchanted Grove—a place bathed in iridescent light, where flora hummed with energy and fauna moved with a graceful elegance. At the heart of the grove stood the Tree of Whispers, its branches laden with silver leaves that shimmered in the moonlight.

The tree beckoned Naziya forward, and as she touched its bark, a surge of ancient wisdom coursed through her veins. She discovered that the grove's magic was intricately tied to the balance of nature and the purity of one's intentions. Naziya's kind heart and genuine curiosity had unlocked the Grove's enchantment, fulfilling the long-awaited prophecy.

News of Naziya's triumph spread throughout Shimla, and the townsfolk celebrated her as a hero. The once-feared Mistwood Forest now became a revered sanctuary, visited by travelers seeking the magic that Naziya had awakened.

As the years passed, Naziya continued to cherish the lessons learned in Mistwood, sharing the tale of her extraordinary journey with the generations that followed. The Enchanted Grove, forever grateful for Naziya's courage, thrived as a testament to the enduring power of curiosity, kindness, and the timeless magic that resides in the hearts of those who dare to embark on extraordinary journeys. And so, the story of Naziya and the Enchanted Grove became a cherished legend, echoing through the ages in the enchanted town of Shimla.

CHAPTER THIRTY-NINE

DAY 39

"IF YOU DON'T LIKE SOMETHING, CHANGE IT. IF YOU CAN'T CHANGE IT, CHANGE YOUR ATTITUDE."

This quote advises proactive change in the face of dissatisfaction. If you dislike something, take action to alter it. When change is impossible, it urges a shift in attitude as a coping mechanism. Whether influencing external circumstances or fostering internal resilience, the message centers on constructive choices. It underscores the power of personal agency and adaptability, emphasizing the importance of actively shaping outcomes or cultivating a positive mindset to navigate challenges effectively. The wisdom lies in recognizing one's capacity to instigate change or, when that's not feasible, embracing a positive perspective to navigate adversity with resilience.

In the vibrant state of Goa, where sun-kissed beaches met the lively streets filled with colorful houses, lived a peculiar bookseller named Ramya. Her charming bookstore, "Ramy Book Store," was a haven for book lovers seeking stories beyond the ordinary.

One balmy afternoon in Goa, a mysterious tome appeared on Ramya's doorstep, bound in faded leather with intricate symbols on its cover. The book seemed to hum with an otherworldly energy. Intrigued, Ramya opened it to find tales of forgotten realms and enchanted worlds.

As Ramya delved into the stories, an ethereal mist enveloped the bookstore, and characters from the book materialized before her. A mischievous pixie, a wise old wizard, and a courageous knight stood in awe of the modern world.

Ramya, ever the adventurer at heart, embraced the magical company and embarked on an extraordinary journey with her newfound friends. Together, they navigated the challenges of both worlds, bridging the gap between reality and fantasy.

As the seasons changed, so did the residents of Goa, who marveled at the wonders unfolding in Ramy Book Store. It became a meeting place for those seeking the extraordinary, a portal to realms where imagination knew no bounds.

The people of Goa, inspired by Ramya's courage, began to pen their own stories, weaving dreams into the fabric of their lives. Goa transformed into a haven for creativity and wonder, proving that sometimes, magic finds its way into the most unexpected places.

And so, the pages of Ramya's story continued to turn, each chapter revealing new adventures, friendships, and the enduring magic that thrived in the heart of Goa—a testament to the power of stories to shape destinies and the boundless possibilities that unfold when one opens a book with a willing heart.

Endnote

Dear Reader,

As you reach the end of "A Mindful Motivational Journey - A Daily Dose of Positive Thinking," I want to express my heartfelt gratitude for accompanying me on this transformative expedition. It has been an honor and a privilege to be a part of your personal growth and to witness the blossoming of your inner light.

Remember, the journey does not end here. This book is merely a catalyst, igniting the flame of positivity, mindfulness, and motivation within you. Now, armed with the insights and tools you have gained, it is time to embark on your own unique path towards a life filled with purpose, joy, and unwavering belief in your potential.

Never underestimate the power of your thoughts and the impact they can have on your reality. Use the tools you have discovered in this book—positive affirmations, mindfulness practices, and resilience-building strategies—to navigate the challenges that lie ahead. Embrace the moments of stillness and gratitude, for they are the fuel that will propel you forward.

Surround yourself with individuals who uplift and inspire you. Share the lessons you have learned with others, for by doing so, you amplify the ripple effect of positivity and motivation in the world. Remember that you have the power to create a ripple that touches countless lives, offering hope and encouragement to those who need it most.

In moments of doubt or adversity, return to the pages of this book. Allow its wisdom to serve as a guiding light, reminding you of the strength and resilience that resides within you. Embrace the challenges as opportunities for growth, knowing that each step you take brings you closer to your dreams.

Always remember that your journey is unique and unfolds at its own pace. Celebrate every small victory along the way and be kind to yourself during moments of setback. It is through these experiences that we learn, evolve, and ultimately thrive.

Finally, I want to acknowledge the immense courage and commitment it takes to embark on a path of personal transformation. By choosing to prioritize your well-being and embrace a positive mindset, you have already taken a remarkable step towards creating a life filled with purpose and fulfillment.

As you venture forth, may your path be adorned with love, resilience, and unwavering belief in your own potential. May you find joy in each moment, strength in each challenge, and inspiration in the beauty that surrounds you. And may you continue to radiate positivity and motivate others with your unwavering spirit.

Thank you for allowing me to be a part of your journey. I wish you all the success and fulfillment that life has to offer.

With heartfelt gratitude,
ANILKUMAR KOLAR RAMESH

www.ingramcontent.com/pod-product-compliance
Lightning Source LLC
Chambersburg PA
CBHW031444150726
47990CB00007B/2593